An Activity Book by
**Devra Newberger Speregen**

Based on the screenplay by
**Robert Rodriguez**

**talk miramax books**

**HYPERION BOOKS FOR CHILDREN**

NEW YORK

Cover photograph by Nels Israelson
Design and illustration by Patrick Merrell
CREATED AND PRODUCED BY PARACHUTE PUBLISHING, L.L.C.


For information address Hyperion Paperbacks for Children,
114 Fifth Avenue, New York, New York 10011-5690

First Edition
1 3 5 7 9 10 8 6 4 2

ISBN:0-7868-1628-7
Library of Congress Catalog Card Number: 00-112177

TOP SECRET!

TOP SECRET!

Carmen and Juni Cortez are two normal kids. They go to school, watch TV, play video games, just like all their friends, until...

...their normal parents are kid-napped by the evil techno-wizard Floop! And then Carmen and Juni find out the truth. Their parents are really secret agents!

•

Floop has created children robots called Spy Kids. He is going to use them to take over the world. But first, he needs to find the all-powerful Third Brain to make his robots smart. And Carmen and Juni's parents have it. As soon as Floop gets the Third Brain, he will turn Mom and Dad into mutants. One thing is clear—Carmen and Juni have to become spies and rescue their parents!

continued

TOP SECRET!

No problem, right? Wrong. Carmen and Juni don't know the first thing about becoming spies. Until they find *the book*. The top secret book their parents left for them. The book that all the world's best spies have been using for centuries. The book called, *How to Be a Spy*.

•

*How to Be a Spy* is filled with super spy tips that help Carmen and Juni slip past their enemies, handle complicated high-tech gadgets, and brave strange and scary mutants.

•

And now Carmen and Juni are going to share the tips and tricks they have learned with you—plus they'll put your spy skills to the test with brain-baffling puzzles and activities. The fact that you are being given access to this top secret information is the first sign that you have the makings of a high-ranking, top-notch secret agent!

TOP SECRET!

# CHAPTER ONE:

## Becoming a Secret Agent

**Secret Spy Tip #1:**

• • • • • • • • • •

**"A Good Spy Uses His or Her Head"**

## Your Secret Agent Profile

Every good spy has a profile. It tells the other spies important and highly confidential (secret) information about that spy.

### AGENT PROFILE

Agent's birth name: ______

Agent's code name: Kirsten

Password: AZyeazyfir

Last known address: 2127498325

Contact e-mail address: ______

e-password: 12567ACD

Hair color: brown    Hair length: 5in.

Eye color: brown    Glasses: Yes ___ No ✓

Height: ______    Weight: ______

Distinguishing marks: ______

DNA sample (strand of hair or spot of saliva):

photo here

Thumbprint:

Your profile information should always be hidden from your enemies. Some of the best hiding places are:

- taped with masking tape to the underside of your bed
- kept in an empty cereal box in a kitchen cabinet (just make sure it's a cereal no one likes!)
- folded over the bottom of a hanger, with clothes hung over it
- placed in the bottom of a puzzle box, covered by all the puzzle pieces

## Outsmarting Your Enemy

Your friends need to give you top secret information. You give them your code name and your password, but how can they be sure it's really you and not someone pretending to be you? Make sure you have a Secret Password Question whose answer only you and your friends know.

For example, your Secret Password Question could be: What is the nickname that your best friend gave you in third grade?

The Secret Password Answer is, of course, Lizard Lips. Only your true friends will know that! So when they ask you the Secret Password Question, if you answer easily with "Lizard Lips," they'll know you can be trusted.

**Your Secret Password Question:**

______________________________

______________________________

______________________________

**Your Secret Password Answer:**

______________________________

## The Perfect Code Name

In the spy world, you are known only by your code name. A code name protects against your enemies finding out your real identity. And with each new mission comes a new code name.

After a while all those code names can get confusing. Here are some ways to choose a code name that will be easy to remember.

• • • • • • •

### Code Name Choice #1:

Pair up your pet's name with the name of the street where you live. For example, if your dog's name is Chip and you live on Willow Street, your code name would be Chip Willow or Willow Chip. If you don't have a pet, try using the name of your friend's or neighbor's pet. Fill in some code names for you and your friends on the next page.

| Person | Pet's Name | Street Name | New Code Name |
| --- | --- | --- | --- |
| Ruby | Sasha | avenue | spakle avenue |
| James | sparkle | avenue | spakleavenue |
| | | | |
| | | | |

**Code Name Choice #2:**

Put together the name of your favorite color with your favorite snack. Some examples are Purple Chips, Red Doodles, and Green Yodels.

| Person | Color | Snack Name | New Code Name |
| --- | --- | --- | --- |
| Sparkle | [illegible] | chips | sprkle |
| | | | |
| | | | |
| | | | |

## What Kind of Spy Are You?

Put your spying smarts to the test and see how you rate as a spy. Are you a super spy, a savvy sleuth, or just an awful agent? Answer the questions below to find out.

1. You're working undercover at a pool party. Your number one suspect is drinking a glass of lemonade, which you know is covered with her fingerprints. You:

   a) Wait until she puts the glass down, then slip on a pair of gloves and secretly switch your glass for hers.
   b) Wait until someone takes her glass away and then go find it.
   c) Ask for a sip of her lemonade and then run away with her glass.

2. What comes next in this pattern?
   CAB DEC EID FOE…

   a) GAB b) GUT c) GUF

3. Can you guess which suspect left these prints in the snow?

a) Suspect #1 b) Suspect #2 c) Suspect #3

4. Your friend says she's going to leave you a secret message on the bathroom mirror at the mall. When you go to look for it, you don't see the message anywhere. What do you do?

a) Figure your friend forgot to leave the message.
b) Sprinkle the mirror with powder to see if the message reappears.
c) Breathe on the mirror to see if the message reappears.

5. You get a message to meet another agent at the park. When you arrive, you see that he's already waiting for you. You:

a) Quietly introduce yourself and secretly pass him the secret information.
b) Give him your code name and ask for the secret password.
c) Shout from across the park, "Yo, Secret Agent! Over here!"

## ANSWERS

1. (a) This is the only answer that won't get other people's fingerprints on the glass.
2. (c) GUF. The first and third letters of each group are in alphabetical order and the middle letters are in vowel order.
3. (a) Suspect #1 walks with a cane. Did you notice his cane print in the snow next to his footprints?
4. (c) The only way to leave a secret mirror message is to write on a steamy mirror. Soon the steam —and the message—will disappear. Breathing on the mirror will make the message reappear.
5. (b) A good spy always exchanges code names and passwords before giving secret information!

## SO HOW DO YOU RATE AS A SPY?

***5 correct answers:*** Congratulations! You're already a super spy. You can make important decisions in the blink of an eye. Use this book to fine-tune your already existing spy skills!

***3-4 correct answers:*** Nice work! You definitely show promise for becoming a savvy sleuth. After you master a few codes, build a few gadgets, and solve some spy puzzles, you'll be ready for anything!

***0-2 correct answers:*** At this point you're a pretty awful agent. But don't worry—we can see your potential! This book is going to show you everything you need to know to become a master spy.

# P•U•Z•Z•L•E•S
## FOR THE SPY-IN-TRAINING

Now you're ready for the ultimate challenge: to test your skills with mind-bending puzzlers! Carmen and Juni put their spy skills to the test with some of the same puzzles found in this book. Grab a pencil, and see how you measure up! (Answers can be found in the back of this book.)

### Hidden Clues

Gregorio Cortez, Carmen and Juni's father, knows it is important to search for clues wherever he goes. Can you find the clues in the sentences below? Look for the words **SPY, SNOOP, HINT, ENEMY, AGENT, MESSAGE, LEAD, SECRET, TRAIL,** and **SEARCH**. Gregorio found the word CODE to get you started.

Example: We have <u>cod e</u>very Saturday night for dinner.

1. He was hit in the chin too much.
2. A gentleman is always kind.
3. Have you met my secretary?
4. Meet Mrs. Krasp, your new teacher.
5. In this winter scene, my snowman is huge!
6. An eagle, a duck, and a bear are at the zoo.
7. There is no operation today.
8. That railing is painted a strange color.
9. The bell next to Brad's ear chimed.
10. Who can work in this mess, a genius?

# Mission Control

Carmen Cortez has been called away for another top secret spy mission. She's left a coded note revealing her new code name. To figure out her new name, write the first letter of the name of each object in the boxes below. Then unscramble the letters to form Carmen's two word code name.

# I Spy

The OSS is the secret international spy agency that Carmen and Juni's parents work for. What does the OSS do? Search for enemy spies. Can you find the word SPIES hidden in this letter grid? It may not look like it, but it's spelled correctly only once in this puzzle! Look up, down, forward, backward, and diagonally.

| | | | | | | | | | |
|---|---|---|---|---|---|---|---|---|---|
| S | S | E | E | S | I | P | S | S | S |
| S | P | I | S | I | P | S | P | I | I |
| P | I | P | I | S | E | S | S | E | S |
| S | S | S | P | P | S | E | I | S | P |
| I | S | S | S | I | S | P | I | S | I |
| E | E | P | E | P | S | S | S | I | E |
| S | S | I | E | I | S | P | E | P | P |
| S | P | S | S | E | P | E | I | S | P |
| S | S | I | P | S | I | S | P | E | S |
| E | P | S | E | S | E | P | I | P | I |

# Word Games

When Carmen first read *How to Be a Spy*, she came across the word ESPIONAGE. Espionage is the act of spying on someone. Can you help her make 15 new words using the letters in the word ESPIONAGE? Write your new words in the spaces provided. After you make 15 words, if you're up for the challenge, try to make 2 seven-letter bonus words!

1 ______________________________

2 ______________________________

3 ______________________________

4 ______________________________

5 ______________________________

6 ______________________________

7 ______________________________

8 ______________________________

9 ______________________________

10 ______________________________

11 ______________________________

12 ______________________________

13 ______________________________

14 ______________________________

15 ______________________________

Bonus: ______________________________

# The Kitchen Mission

When Carmen and Juni's parents are kidnapped, the Cortez kids are whisked away to the high-tech OSS safe house for protection. In the safe house, Carmen finds some strange looking packets of food, but she can't figure out how to cook them. Unscramble the letters on each packet to spell the name of each food. Then put the numbered letters in the spaces below to learn how food is prepared in the safe house.

**The food goes in the** __ __ __ __ __ __ __ __ __ __
1 2 3 4 5 6 7 8 9 10

TTSPIHGEA
8
DFIRE
KCCNEIH
3
EIRC
NDA
SBANE
1
STCAO
7
NTPAEU TTBRUE
DAN LELYJ
10
4

# CHAPTER TWO:

## Make Your Own Spy Kit

**Secret Spy Tip #2:**
**• • • • • • • • • •**
**"A Good Spy Is Always Prepared"**

There's no question that you need smarts to become an ace agent. But you also need something else: a fully loaded spy kit on hand for just about every emergency!

Juni always carries his lunch box spy kit handcuffed to his wrist when he's on a mission. His uncle Machete is a professional spy gadget inventor, and he helped Juni make many of the gadgets in his kit. But you can make a lot of the same stuff at home using items found around the house.

First, you'll need to find something to hold all your spy gadgets. You can use an old lunch box, or if you don't have one, use a small backpack or even a shoe box. (Be sure to tie a string around the shoe box so none of your gadgets fall out!)

**Once you have a spy kit, you're ready to fill it up with all your spy necessities. Here's a list of spy tools that Carmen and Juni never leave home without.**

# Spy Putty

Spy putty has lots of uses. You can use it to jam a keyhole if you don't want to be spied on while making secret plans. Spy putty can also be used to hide small objects under your bed (or anyplace else). Just stick the object to the spy putty and stick the putty to the underside of your bed!

***To Make Spy Putty You'll Need:***

- 1/2 cup white glue
- 1 cup water
- 1 tbsp. laundry borax (found in any grocery store)
- 2 medium-size plastic containers
- 2 drops food coloring
- a plastic bag

***Here's How to Make It:***

1. Add 1/2 cup water and 1/2 cup glue to a plastic container. Stir.

2. Mix in a few drops food coloring.

3. In the second container, mix 1 tbsp. borax and 1/2 cup water. Stir.

4. Add the borax mixture to the glue mixture. The putty should form instantly. Store in a plastic bag.

## Spy Pencil

You will use your spy pencil to keep track of clues and write coded messages. Pencils are better than pens, because if you make a mistake, pencil marks are easy to erase.

## White Paper

Keep a few sheets of white paper on hand at all times. White paper is always needed to write secret messages and take notes. It is the only color that can be used with different kinds of invisible ink.

## Invisible Ink

***To Make Invisible Ink You'll Need:***

- a lemon wedge (in a sealed plastic bag)
- small paper cup
- toothpicks

***Here's How to Make It:***

1. Squeeze the juice from the lemon into the paper cup. This is your ink.

2. Dip a toothpick into the ink and start writing your message on the white paper. You'll have to dip often—probably a few dips for each letter you write. When you've finished, leave the paper to dry for a few minutes.

3. To read your message, hold the paper near BUT NOT TOO CLOSE TO a lightbulb. Your invisible message should appear in just a few seconds.

## Birthday Candle

Pack a white birthday candle in your spy kit for writing invisible messages. Using the candle as a pencil, write your message on a piece of white paper. The paper will look blank. But the message will appear if you sprinkle the paper with pepper, dirt, or any fine dark powder.

## Snoopscope

This is the ultimate snooping machine—and it's simple to make.

***To Make a Snoopscope You'll Need:***

- 2 half-gallon milk or juice cartons
- scissors or a craft knife
- 2 mirrors, 1 1/2 by 2 1/2 inches (found at drugstores)
- masking tape

***Here's How to Make It:***

1. Wash out the empty cartons with water. Dry. Then use scissors or a craft knife to cut the tops off the cartons.

2. Cut an fist-size hole in the side of each carton about 1 inch up from the bottom.

3. In both cartons, use masking tape to tape a mirror, reflective side up, inside the carton, 2 inches from the bottom. The mirror should be taped to the carton wall opposite the small hole.

4. Press the tops of the cartons together and secure them with masking tape. It is important to make sure that the viewing holes you cut out of each carton are on opposite sides of the snoopscope after you tape the tops of the cartons together.

5. Look into one of the viewing holes. The mirrors will allow you to see out the other end! Say you want to look around a corner but don't want anyone to see you. Stand against a wall. Hold the snoopscope so that the other end sticks out past the corner. Then look into your end of the scope, and you'll be able to see around the corner!

## Locating Device

Back when your grandparents were kids — before all spy gadgets were electronic, spies used compasses to locate which direction they were heading in.

That way, they wouldn't bump into their enemies. A compass is a gadget that uses an arrow to tell you which way is north. By knowing which way is north, you will always know whether you are heading north, south, east, or west.

***To Make a Locating Device You'll Need:***

- a plastic container with a lid
- water
- a small chunk of Styrofoam, about 1/4 the size of your container (a packaging peanut is perfect!)
- a magnet
- a sewing needle

***Here's How to Make It:***

1. Fill half of the plastic container with water.
2. Float the Styrofoam in the water.
3. Pick up the magnet in one hand and the needle in the other. Stroke the needle along one end of the magnet 20 times, going in the same direction with each stroke.
4. Gently place the needle on top of the Styrofoam. Watch how the Styrofoam moves. It should circle around until it points north.

To travel with your locating device, remove the Styrofoam and needle from the bowl and keep in a sealed plastic bag in your spy kit. Seal in the water with the container's lid, and you're good to go…in any direction!

# Pink Fizz Bombs

Pink Fizz Bombs are perfect for creating a diversion, so a spy can slip through a crowd unnoticed. Toss one onto the ground and slink away as the bomb explodes! You can be sure no one will be watching you!

***To Make Pink Fizz Bombs You'll Need:***

- Ziploc bag
- 1 1/2 tbsp. baking soda
- a paper towel
- 1/2 cup warm water
- 1/2 cup vinegar
- a few drops red food coloring

***Here's How to Make Them:***

1. Check your Ziploc bag for holes by filling with water and zipping closed. Turn over a few times to check for leaks. Spill out water.

2. Place 1 1/2 tbsp. baking soda in the center of a paper towel.

3. Fold the paper towel in squares to make a small packet for the baking soda.

4. Put 1/2 cup vinegar and 1/2 cup warm water in the empty Ziploc bag. Add two drops red food coloring.

5. Zip the bag shut and take it outdoors to where you want to create your diversion. When you reach the spot, open the bag and drop in the paper towel with the baking soda. You have a couple of seconds to zip the bag closed tightly before it activates. Give the bag a shake and toss to the ground. When it activates, you'll have a pink mini-explosion as the bag fizzes and pops!

# Electro Shock Gumballs

Carmen and Juni never go on a mission without a few electro shock gumballs tucked into their spy kits. Here's Uncle Machete's recipe for homemade electro shock gumballs. They're best when chewed in the dark—and are sure to catch your enemy off guard!

***To Make Electro Shock Gumballs You'll Need:***

- wintergreen breath mints
- a piece of bubble gum (the kind that makes big bubbles)

***Here's How to Make Them:***

1. Take a piece of bubble gum and wrap it around a mint.
2. Turn off the lights and crunch down.
3. Watch the sparks fly—and the surprised expression on everyone's faces!

# Transmogrification Ooze

Impress all your spy friends with this ooze that morphs from solid to liquid and back to solid in the blink of an eye.

***To Make Transmogrification Ooze You'll Need:***

- newspaper
- 1 cup dry cornstarch
- a mixing bowl
- a few drops food coloring
- 1/2 cup water

***Here's How to Make It:***

1. Cover your work space with newspaper.

2. Pour the cornstarch into the bowl.

3. Add a drop or two food coloring.

4. Slowly mix in the water with your fingers. Keep adding water until the cornstarch turns liquidy. Test the mixture by tapping it. When it doesn't splash, it's ready!

5. Roll the mixture into a ball. Then let it sit in your hand and watch what happens. In seconds it begins to change to a liquid and ooze through your fingers. Roll it around in your palms, and you'll have a solid substance again!

# Help Wanted at Machete's Spy Shop

Uncle Machete is always searching for new inventions to sell in his spy shop. What super high-tech gadget would you create for him?

***My own secret spy invention is called:***

***Here's what it does:***

***Here's how to make it:***

# P•U•Z•Z•L•E•S FOR THE SPY-IN-TRAINING

Carmen and Juni rely on high-tech gadgets for expert spying. But they know you also need brains—and we're not talking about the fake ones created by Floop. Put your brain to the test and see how many of Carmen's and Juni's favorite puzzles you can master!

## Confidential: For Your Eyes Only

Gregario and Ingrid Cortez have collected many spy secrets over the years. Put the numbered words in order to find out two of their biggest ones.

| HE (9) | FROM (5) | LASER (3) |
|---|---|---|
| BEAMS (4) | SHE (1) | HIS (17) |
| SHOOTS (2) | IN (16) | FINGERNAILS (8) |
| A (11) | KEEPS (10) | FILE (14) |
| METAL (13) | MUSTACHE (18) | THIN (12) |
| HIDDEN (15) | UNDER (6) | HER (7) |

Ingrid's secret:

________ ________ ________ ________
1 2 3 4

________ ________ ________ ________.
5 6 7 8

Gregorio's secret:

________ ________ ________ ________ ________
9 10 11 12 13

________ ________ ________ ________
14 15 16 17

________.
18

# Password Puzzler

Carmen doesn't want Juni, her little brother, snooping around her stuff, so she always keeps her spy kit locked. The only way to open it is to say the password. See if you can help Juni figure out Carmen's password.

Start at the arrow and go around the circle twice in a clockwise direction, putting every other letter from the circle in the spaces provided. Then use the numbered letters to spell out Carmen's password.

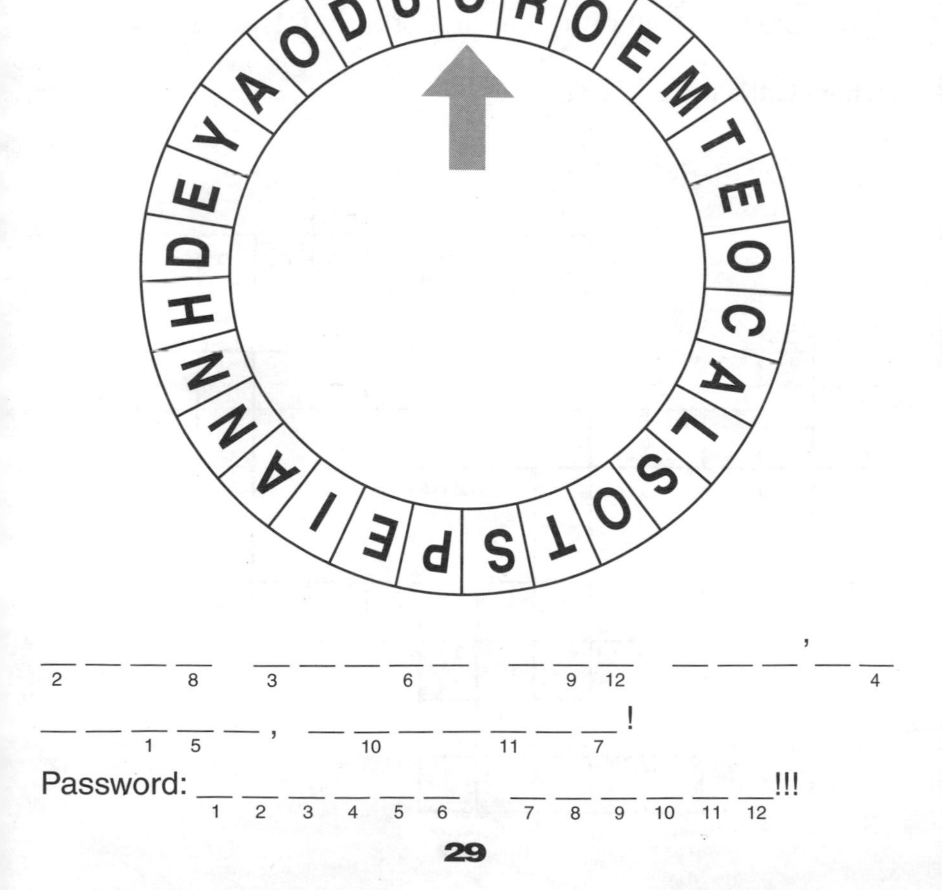

# Picture This

Miss Gradenko and her agents are searching the safe house for the Third Brain. She wants to find it before Carmen and Juni so she can impress her boss, Floop. With her mini-camera, she snaps photos all throughout the safe house but the Third Brain is nowhere to be found.

First, write the name of each picture on the next page underneath the picture, then into the boxes in the grid below. There is only one way all the names will fit! When the grid is complete, put the numbered letters from the boxes in the numbered spaces below. It will spell out the location of the Third Brain. We've done the first one to get you started.

**Where is the Third Brain?** ___ ___ ___ ___ ___ ___   ___
1 2 3 4 5 6 7

___ ___ ___ ___ ___ ___ ___ ___ ___ ___
8 9 10 11 12 13 14 15 16 17

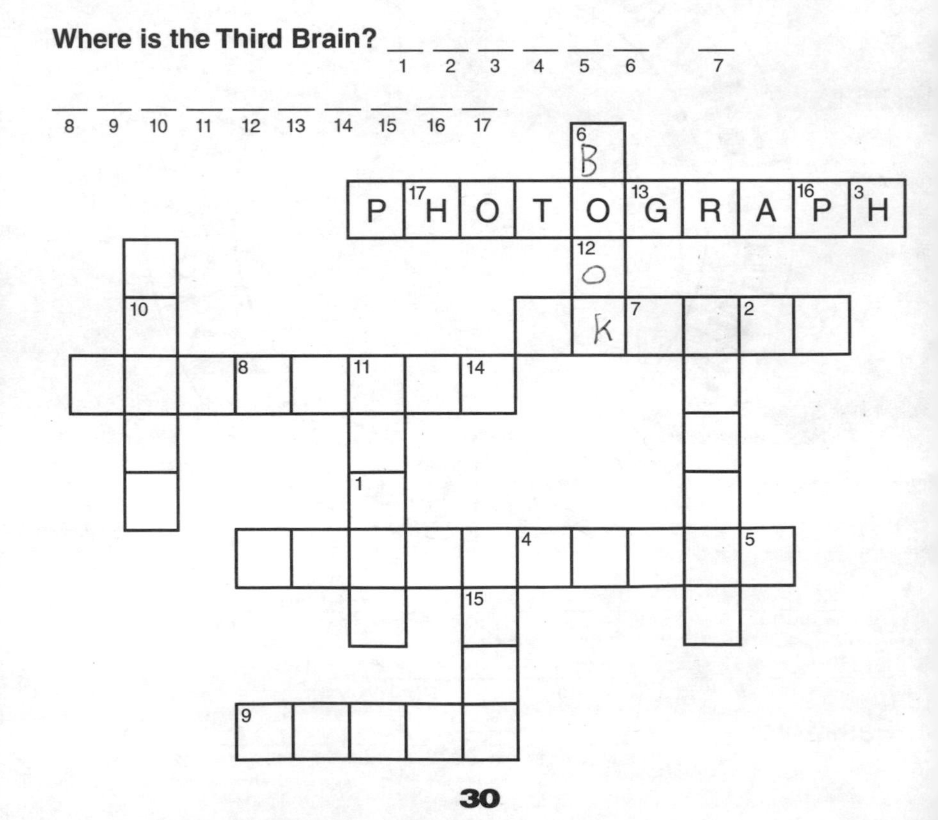

PHOTOGRAPH
books
House

# Tell It Like It Is

Uncle Felix has been leaving the Cortez family some crazy messages. Can you crack the code and figure out what they mean?

a. SEARCHING CLUES
CLUES
CLUES
CLUES

b. surveillance
UR

c. forMISSINGmation

d. AGENTAGENT

e. MEthey're

f. CROSS
CROSS

g. **TELLcounterIGENCE**

h. **COVER**
**Working**

i. **co de**

j. **INK**

k. **D**
**R E**
**E C**
**D O**

a._________________________________________

b._________________________________________

c._________________________________________

d._________________________________________

e._________________________________________

f._________________________________________

g._________________________________________

h._________________________________________

i._________________________________________

j._________________________________________

k._________________________________________

# All Thumbs

The Thumb Thumbs are leaving their thumbprints all over the place! Follow the paths through each thumbprint maze below. Each path will form a letter that spells out what person the Thumb Thumbs love the most.

Answer:

____ ____ ____ ____ ____
1 2 3 4 5

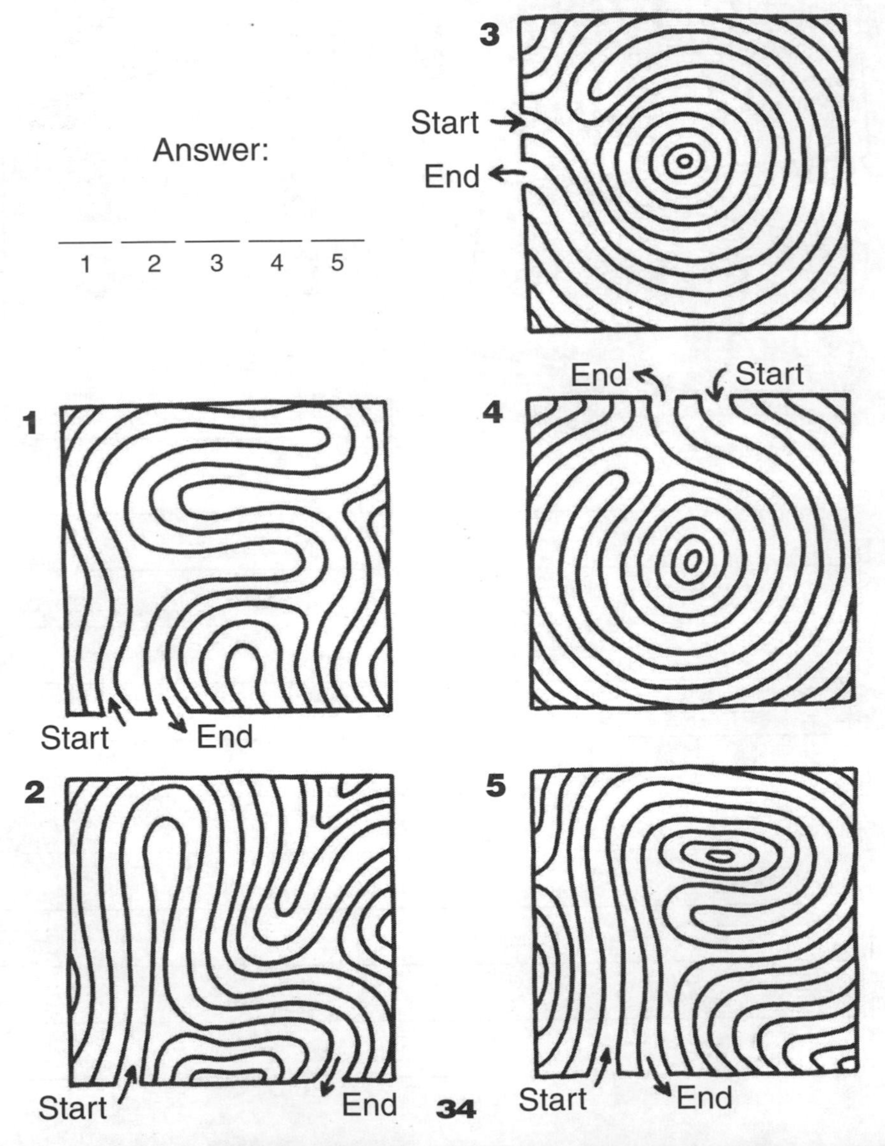

# S.O.S. for the OSS!

Alexander Minion is Floop's evil sidekick. His phony OSS ring has become mixed up with some real OSS rings. Find the fake by crossing out all the lowercase letters and even numbers. When you see what you're left with, the impostor will be obvious!

# CHAPTER THREE:

## Master of Disguise

**Secret Spy Tip #3:**
**• • • • • • • • • •**
**"A Good Spy Can Blend into His or Her Surroundings"**

So you want to look like a spy. What do you wear, a big sign on your shirt that says "spy?"

Of course not! Part of being a good spy is making sure that no one knows you're a spy. A secret agent must be able to sneak, slip through, climb over, and slink around anything. A secret agent also has to "shadow" his suspects — which means following them very closely without being noticed. So the clothing you wear should blend in with your surroundings. Here are some of Carmen's and Juni's tips on...

## How to Dress Like a Spy

- **Be practical**. Wear dark colors at night, and that means socks too! Dress in regular clothes (like jeans and a T-shirt) when you're spying during the day. You'll stand out like a sore Thumb Thumb if you're dressed in all-black spy gear!

- **Be creative**. Every article of clothing you wear can have a double purpose. A belt, jacket lining, or cuff is an excellent hiding place. Sneakers or baseball caps make great message carriers.

- **Be aware**. If you are going to be spying at the ski lodge, wear ski clothes. Don't show up at the beach without your bathing suit. Think in advance about where you are going and what people will be wearing and doing. This way you won't stand out or seem suspicious.

### 5 Easy Ways to Change Your Look

1. Always carry bubble gum with you. Nothing covers your face better than a giant pink bubble!
2. Change your hairstyle. Wear a wig, throw on a hat, or even part your hair differently.
3. Glasses, an eye patch, or a fake mustache and beard are a fun and easy way to hide your face.
4. Wearing multiple layers of clothing can make you look heavier than you really are.
5. Change your walk. Start limping. Add a swagger to your step. Slouch if you normally stand up straight. Believe it or not, this will make a big difference in your appearance.

## How to Talk Like a Spy

Disguise your voice. It's fun to do and important for a spy-in-training to learn. Here are some easy ways to change the way you talk:

- **Adopt a foreign accent**. You can perfect your accent by listening to people you know or people on TV who have that accent.
- **Speak with a higher or lower pitch**.
- **Hold your nose while you talk.** This may not work in person, but it's great for phone conversations.

• **Keep your conversations short!** The less you speak, the less chance someone has to recognize you. Also, if you keep your conversations short, you're less likely to slip out of your new voice.

## Secret Languages

Another way to speak like a spy is to invent a secret language of your own. Grab a friend and learn the languages below.

### ★ Opposite Talk ★

This is a fun way to disguise your conversation and confuse everyone around you. Replace as many words or phrases as you can with their opposite meaning. For example, instead of saying, "Meet me before school at my house," you would tell your friend, "Meet you after school at your house."

### ★ Pig Latin ★

You may sound silly at first, but once you get the hang of Pig Latin, you can speak it for hours. The key is removing the first letter of each word and adding it to the end of that word, followed by the sound "ay." For example, "Hello" in Pig Latin would be, "Ellohay." "Please pass the cookies" would be "Leasepay asspay hetay ookiescay."

# P•U•Z•Z•L•E•S
## FOR THE SPY-IN-TRAINING

Nice work so far — Carmen and Juni would be proud! You've learned to think like a spy, move like a spy, and talk like a spy. Now it's time to take on the super spy puzzles.

### Bad Guys, Beware!

The villains listed below are all welcome guests at Floop's castle. Look for them in the word search below. Look up, down, forward, backward, and diagonally.

| | | |
|---|---|---|
| FOOGLIES | MR. LISP | ALEXANDER MINION |
| FLOOP | MISS GRADENKO | THUMB THUMBS |

F N A F N U X E D R E F R S N
V G T U F L I S E I L G O O F
L F H A Y A Q U T Y F H I P A
N I M I S S G R A D E N K O A
O O N S M M N G U R I G Z O I
I V T M B L K Q C M I F G L S
T N U B M M F E R T S Z S F M
K J A X O J U E B I N E O L P
W E D G O I D H A X O N O A T
K R N E F N H F T O N D P H S
N G A F A G P N K B O O C E T
O F L X X P S I L R M R Q F U
I B E N A N X E D E F U F W V
M L D W O I E X A Z E F H A D
A C D E R M P Y L N G E B T X

# Will the Real Carmen Please Stand Up?

Carmen is on a top secret mission, and she is in disguise. Can you figure out which girl is Carmen, using the clues below? Change one letter in each of the underlined words to understand the clue better.

Here's an example to get you started: Carmen's pig is not dark. Change one letter of "pig" to "wig." Now you know that Carmen has a light colored wig.

**Clues:**

- Carmen's skirt is long-sleeved.
- Carmen is not wearing books.
- Carmen has classes on her face.
- Carmen is not wearing a map.
- Carmen is carrying a bug.

# Super Guppy Getaway

The Super Guppy is racing through the ocean toward the safe house. Can you get it safely through the maze before it is stopped by Floop's evil henchmen?

# HOW TO DRAW A FOOGLIE

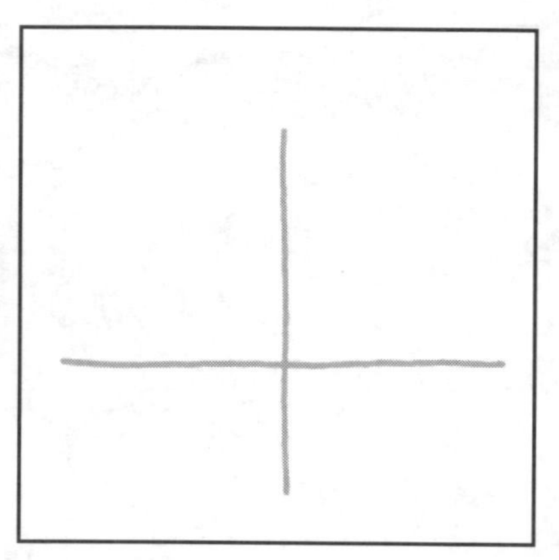

1. Using a pencil, draw a cross. The line going across should be a little below center.

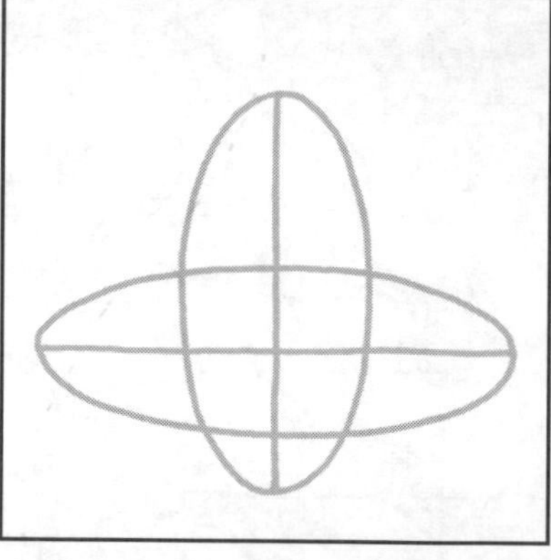

2. Draw a flat oval around each of the lines. The cross and ovals will be your main guidelines.

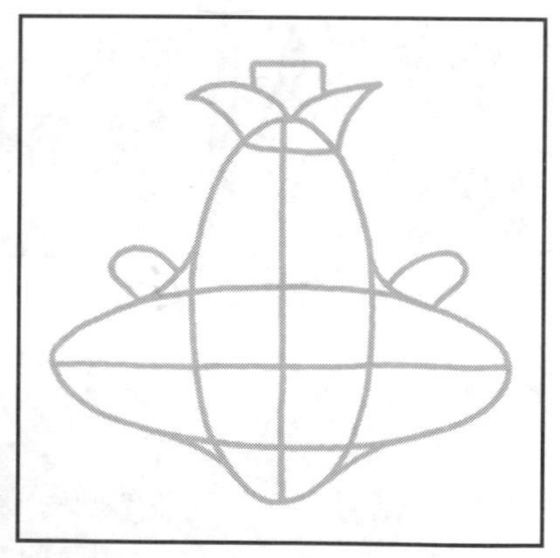

3. Sketch in the guidelines for the ears and hat. Add 4 curved guidelines to connect the ovals.

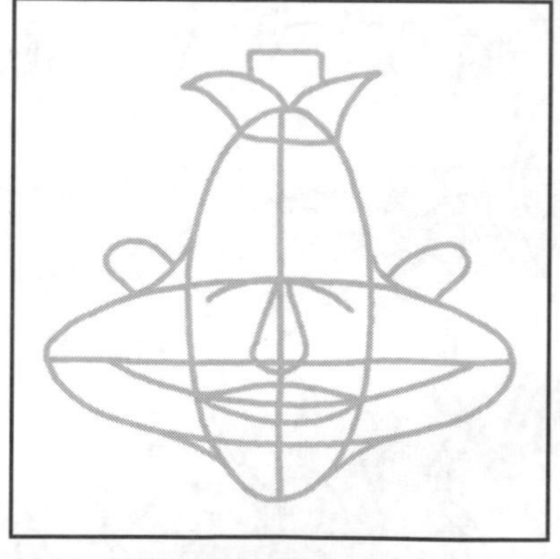

4. Using the cross and ovals as your guide, sketch in the mouth, eyes and nose.

Juni's favorite characters on TV are the Fooglies. He even drew a Fooglie of his own. Want to learn how you can draw a Fooglie, too? Here's how:

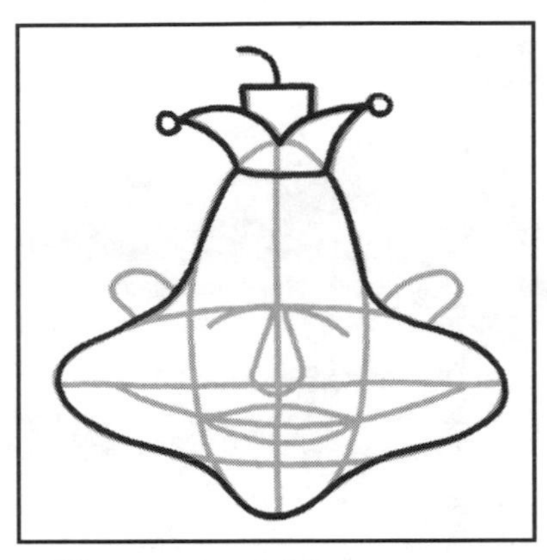

5. Time to use ink!
Carefully trace the hat and head guidelines with your pen.

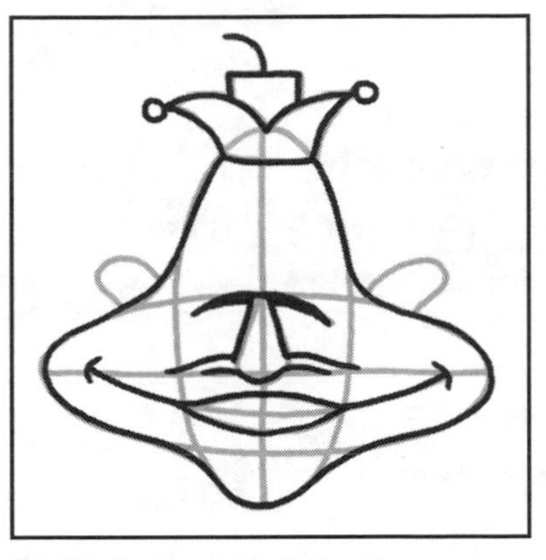

6. Next, draw the mouth, eyes, and nose as shown.

7. Add teeth, draw in the ears, and add a few wrinkles on the forehead.

8. Erase all your pencil lines and you've just drawn your own Fooglie!

# Now You See It, Now You Don't

Can you figure out the message Floop's boss, Mr. Lisp, has written to Floop? Believe it or not, it *isn't* written in code! *HINT: It isn't what the message says, but how you look at it.*

# Cable Collision

Floop's evil Spy Kids have gotten their jet pack cables twisted. Can you figure out which cable belongs to which jet pack?

# A Top-Flight Mission

Machete's Spy Shop has the latest technology in spy gear. But Uncle Machete has just one all-important super-fast vehicle. Do you know what it is? First find all the gadgets and vehicles in the word search on the next page. Look up, down, forward, backward, and diagonally. The letters that haven't been circled (starting at the top and going across each row) will spell out the answer.

***Look for these words:***

SPY WATCHES
WRIST COMMUNICATORS
LOCATOR DEVICES
JET PACKS
SUPER GUPPY
TRACKING DEVICE
SPY KITS
SURVEILLANCE CAMERA
TELEPHONE TAPS
HDTV COMPACTS
MINI-CAMERAS
ACID CRAYONS
MICRO-COMPUTERS
LASERS
SPY GLASSES
FLIGHT SIMULATORS
DIGITAL SCREENS

U S R E T U P M O C O R C I M
N A K C S E H C T A W Y P S L
E R M C A C H E T E R E H A H
S E O N A L Y O N E I C B D F
D M E S I P J I N G S I T E L
I A X E P S T R E S T V S S I
G C T S I A N E H I C E S E G
I E E S S R P Y J O O D S C H
T C L A H E O P M T M G H I T
A N E L E M F P A S M N T V S
L A P G E A A S S T U I L E I
S L H Y A C N D R S N K E D M
C L O P T I A A E N I C D R U
R I N S A N I R S V C A E O L
E E H I I C L A E A R I T A
E V T N T M H E L S T T P A T
N R A C I D C R A Y O N S C O
S U P E R G U P P Y R Y W O R
O S S R S T I K Y P S L D L S

**Answer:** ______ _________

___ _____ ___

_________ _________

__ ___ ___ _____-___

_________ _____, ___

___ ____ _________

__ ____ ____ ________!

# Danger Ahead!

Carmen and Juni have made it to the underwater entrance to Floop's castle, but they can't get inside. Connect the dots to see what's in their way!

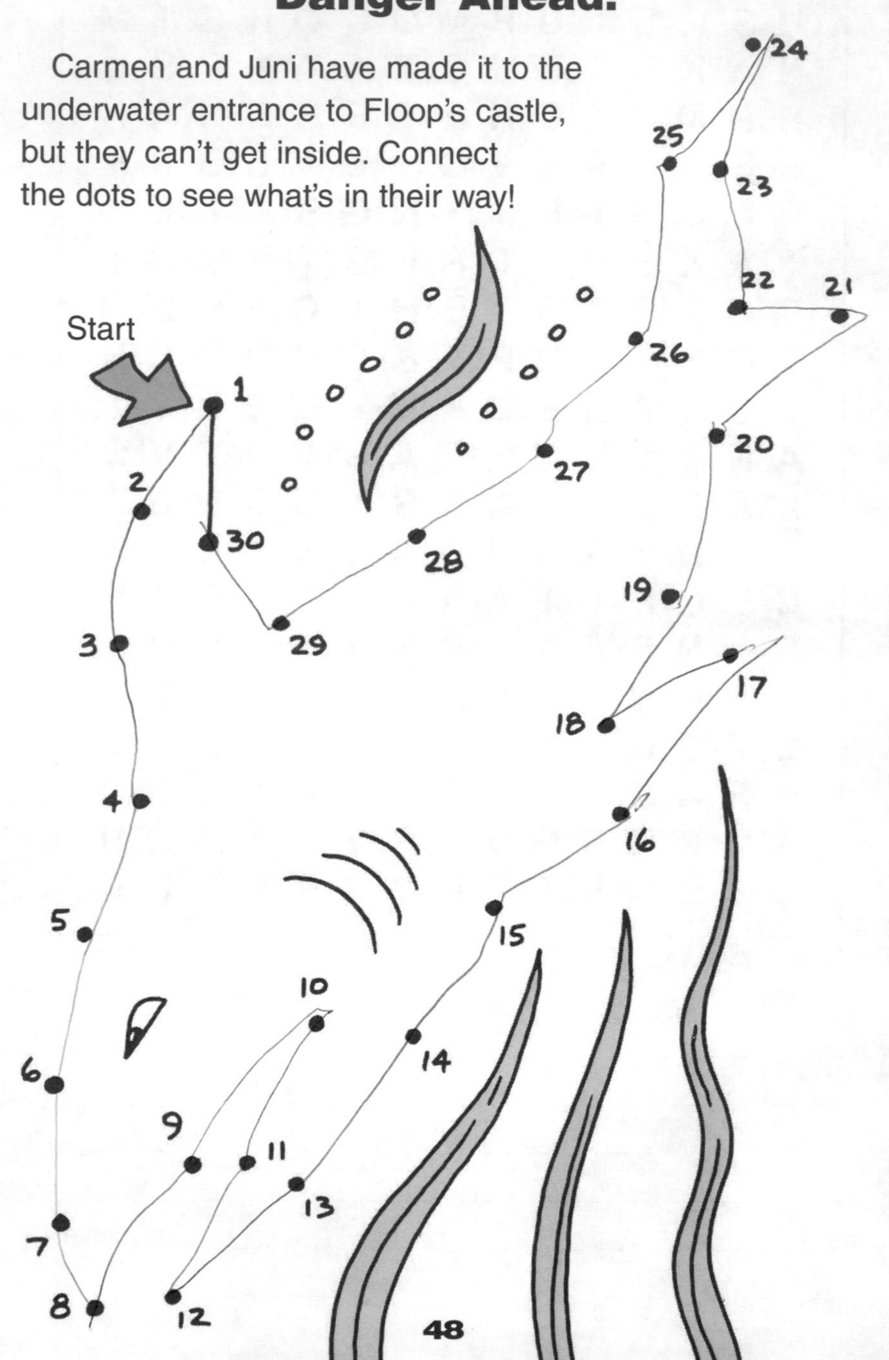

# Thumbs Up!

Floop's castle is filled with evil Thumb Thumbs. Can you find the 10 THUMBS in this search?

| | | | | | | | |
|---|---|---|---|---|---|---|---|
| U | S | B | M | U | H | T | T |
| H | T | M | S | S | U | H | T |
| T | H | U | M | B | S | U | H |
| S | S | M | B | M | B | M | H |
| B | B | T | H | U | M | B | S |
| M | U | M | H | H | U | S | U |
| U | M | B | U | T | H | T | M |
| S | B | M | U | H | T | S | H |
| S | B | M | U | H | T | B | B |
| H | T | T | H | U | M | B | S |
| S | S | M | T | H | U | B | T |

# CHAPTER FOUR:

## Cracking Codes

**Secret Spy Tip #4:**

• • • • • • • • • •

**"A Good Spy Uses Deception in Place of Force"**

Deception is a big part of being a spy. It means sneaking around and fooling your enemies. A good example of how a spy uses deception is when he or she writes a message in secret code. Notes written in secret codes look like nonsense to most people but mean something important to the spy who receives them! All a spy needs to crack a code is a code key. A code key tells you how to decipher the code.

Here are eight of Carmen's and Juni's favorite secret codes. Some are harder to learn than others, but with a little practice you can easily memorize them in just a short time. When you've mastered these codes, why not try inventing a few of your own?

CODES

# Secret Code #1: Backward Alphabet Code

Let's start off with the most basic code. The Backward Alphabet Code is so easy that it is often used as part of a double code (you will learn about these later in this chapter).

***Here's How the Code Works:***

First, make a code key so you know how to decipher the code. Write the alphabet down the side of a piece of paper in a column. Then, next to what you've written, write the alphabet in a column again, only backward this time, starting with Z. Your Backward Alphabet Code Key should look like this ⟶

A - Z
B - Y
C - X
D - W
E - V
F - U
G - T
H - S
I - R
J - Q
K - P
L - O
M - N
N - M
O - L
P - K
Q - J
R - I
S - H
T - G
U - F
V - E
W - D
X - C
Y - B
Z - A

Next, when writing your secret message, switch the letters in the second column for the letters in the first column. In Backward Alphabet Code, the words SECRET AGENT would look like this: HVXIVG ZTVMG. As you can see on your code key, S=H, E=V, C=X, and so on. Got the hang of it? Try writing your code name in Backward Alphabet Code:

______________________________

# CODE #1 (WITH A TWIST)

A way to put a cool twist on the Backward Alphabet Code is to use a "key letter." This means you start writing the backwards alphabet on your code key at a letter other than A. For example, if your key letter is G your code key would look like this:

Start lettering backward here at key letter G → G - Z

A - F
B - E
C - D
D - C
E - B
F - A
G - Z
H - Y
I - X
J - W
K - V
L - U
M - T
N - S
O - R
P - Q
Q - P
R - O
S - N
T - M
U - L
V - K
W - J
X - I
Y - H
Z - G

Now what does your code name look like in this code?

______________________________

# Secret Code #2: The Number Code

Another code often used by top-ranking spies is the Number Code. Simply substitute a number from 1 to 26 for each letter:

A - 1
B - 2
C - 3
D - 4
E - 5
F - 6
G - 7
H - 8
I - 9
J - 10
K - 11
L - 12
M - 13
N - 14
O - 15
P - 16
Q - 17
R - 18
S - 19
T - 20
U - 21
V - 22
W - 23
X - 24
Y - 25
Z - 26

CODE #2

SECRET AGENT in the Number Code reads:
19-5-3-18-5-20 1-7-5-14-20.
Write your best friend's code name in Number Code:

______________________________

# Secret Code #3: The Symbol Code

A really smart spy might figure out the patterns in the first two codes. But here's one that no spy will be able to crack without the top secret code key. The Symbol Code substitutes symbols for letters. When you write secret messages, you can use the code below or create your own symbols. Just make sure you and all your spy partners have the same code key!

SECRET AGENT in Symbol Code looks like this:

”%#?%■ !✓%¢■

See if you can write your favorite hiding place in Symbol Code:

______________________________

**A - !**
**B - ☆**
**C - #**
**D - $**
**E - %**
**F - ^**
**G - ✓**
**H - ***
**I - (**
**J - )**
**K - _**
**L - +**
**M - =**
**N - ¢**
**O - ▲**
**P - }**
**Q - /**
**R - ?**
**S - ”**
**T - ■**
**U - :**
**V - <**
**W - >**
**X - [**
**Y - ]**
**Z - ♥**

# Secret Code #4: Tic-Tac-Toe Code

Is it alien handwriting or a secret code? That's what your enemies will be trying to figure out — but you'll know how to read it. The Tic-Tac-Toe Code looks like the following:

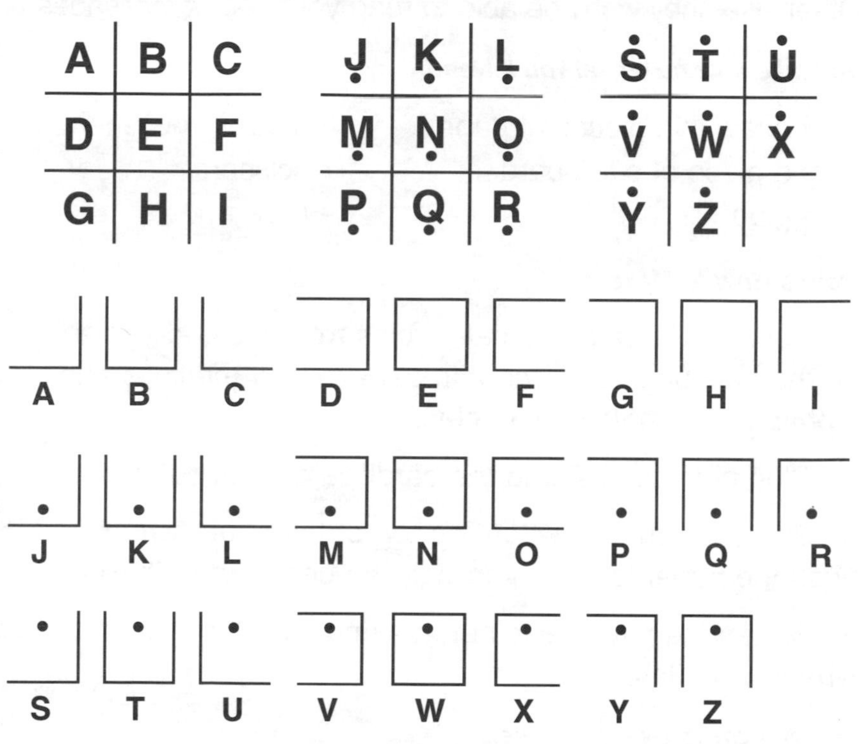


To write in Tic-Tac-Toe code, use the section of the grid that your letter is in instead of the letter itself. For example, the letter A would look like this:

SECRET AGENT written in Tic-Tac-Toe Code would look like this:

Can you write your favorite disguise in Tic-Tac-Toe Code?

# Secret Code #5: Code Wheel Code

The Code Wheel is a must-have for every good agent's spy kit. It forms many different code keys with a turn of the wheel. (Make sure that your spy partners all have code wheels, too. Otherwise, they won't be able to read your secret messages.)

***To Make a Code Wheel You'll Need:***

- a few thin pieces of paper
- a piece of cardboard
- glue
- a paper fastener
- scissors
- a pen

***Here's How to Make It:***

1. Trace the large and small circles from the code wheel on the next page onto the thin paper. Copy the lines and alphabet onto both your circles.
2. Glue both circles onto the cardboard, then cut them out.
3. Place the smaller wheel on top of the larger wheel and push the paper fastener through the center of both wheels.
4. Fasten the paper fastener, making sure that the small wheel can rotate.

***Here's How to Use the Wheel:***

Choose a key letter, like you did with the Backward Alphabet Code (any letter but A). Turn the small wheel until this key letter matches up with the letter A on the larger wheel. Now just switch the letters on the smaller wheel for the ones on the bigger wheel when writing your message. If you match up J on the inside wheel to A on the larger wheel, what would your favorite hiding place look like in this code?

________________________________________

Z A B C D E F G H I J K L M N O P Q R S T U V W X Y
CODE #5
Z A B C D E F G H I J K L M N O P Q R S T U V W X Y
CODE
WHEEL

## Secret Code #6: Under-Over Code

This is a code that looks really complicated to solve, but it's actually easy — if you know what you're doing.

***Here's How It Works:***

1. Decide on the sentence you want to write. Let's use THE SECRET'S OUT as an example. Then take a piece of paper and draw a line dividing the top half of the paper from the bottom half.

2. Write your message, one letter above the other on the line, like this:

| T E E R T O T |
|---|
| H S C E S U |

3. Then, on a separate piece of paper, write the two new "words" next to each other like this:

**Teertot Hscesu**

4. Now send the message to the other spies. All they have to do to decode it is put the first word on top of the second and read up and down.

What is your secret password in Under-Over Code?

---

## Secret Code #7: The Pencil Wrap

You can use the pencil in your spy kit for creating and cracking this clever code. Just make sure that your spy partner has the same size pencil in his or her spy kit to decode the message. You will also need a strip of paper about 1/2 inch wide, scissors, and some tape.

***Here's How It Works:***

Tape one end of the paper strip near the eraser of the pencil. Carefully wind the paper all the way down the pencil. When you reach the pencil point, tape down the other end of the paper strip. Then write your message in a straight line going down the pencil.

Untape the paper strip and unwind it. Your message will be completely scrambled—until your friend winds it around his pencil and gets the secret info!

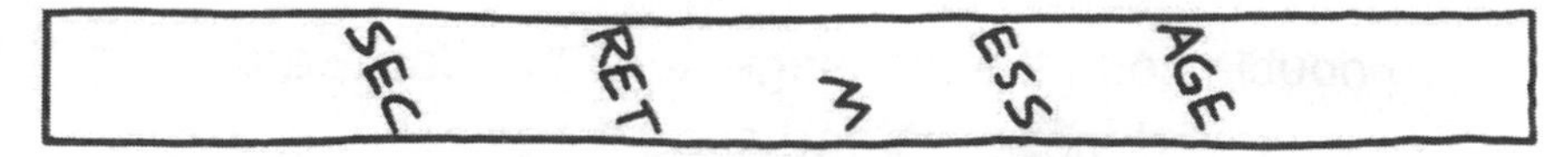


## Secret Code #8: Broken Code

You have thirty seconds to write and send a secret message to a fellow agent before you're captured by the enemy. What are you going to do? Use the Broken Code—it's the easiest code to create and the hardest code to crack!

Here is a sentence written in Broken Code:

**Ca nyouc rac kthi sco de?**

No, it's not written in a foreign language. The words are just split in the wrong places. It says: Can you crack this code?

Write the name of your secret meeting place in Broken Code:

_______________________________________________

## CODE #8

_______________________________________________

## Double Coding

Since there are many experienced code crackers out there, no message you send is 100 percent safe. That's why it's a good idea to double code your message.

For example, you send the message MEET ME LATER using the Backward Alphabet code. It looks like this: NVVG NV OZGVI.

To double code the message, take the Backward Alphabet-coded message and code it again. For example, NVVG NV OZGVI in Symbol Code looks like this: ¢ < < ✓ ¢ < ▲♥✓< (

You and your partner should agree in advance on the two codes you will write messages in. That way, if an enemy somehow cracks the Symbol Code in your message, all their message will say is NVVG NV OZGVI! But your friend will know to use the Backward Alphabet Code next for the real message!

# L•E•T'S G•E•T C•R•A•C•K•I•N•G

## Codes From A to Z

Carmen and Juni have sent you a top secret message. Use the Backward Alphabet Code to decipher it.

**Z TLLW HKB ZODZBH FHVH XLWVH!**

Message:________________________________________

## The Ultimate Brain Baffler

Juni loves brain teasers. This is his favorite one:

**Q:** What does a good spy always seek out?

The answer is written in Number Code:

**A:** 20-8-5 14-13-5 Answer:__ __ __ __ __ __

(If you're still baffled, turn to the answer key on page 79.)

## TV Signals

The Fooglies may sing and dance on Floop's TV show, but if you hear their songs backward, it has a double meaning. Crack the double code to find out what secret message they are sending to Floop's TV viewers. Use the Tic-Tac-Toe Code to decipher the first part, then use the Backward Alphabet Code to finish it off.

Decoding 1:__ __ __ __ __ __ Decoding 2:__ __ __ __ __ __!

# Double Trouble

Carmen and Juni are zooming across the sky with their jet packs, searching the city for their Spy Kid doubles. When they separate to cover more territory, Juni leaves coded messages for Carmen all over the city. Start at Ukressa's Department Store and help Carmen follow Juni's trail to see where he found the robot doubles. Use the different code keys in the beginning of this chapter to help you crack each code.

The robot doubles were hiding at the:

________________________________________

POLICE
R ULFMW
GSVN!
HOSPITAL
AL'S SUPERMARKET
Ha dtog o.
Imhe ade dfo
rthep oli cest
ati on.
AL'S
SALE

# The Name of the Game

Carmen's full name is a password used all over the world! To find out Carmen's full name, start at the circled letter in the center ring. Read the letters in a clockwise direction around the ring, then jump to the next ring and do the same thing. Always start with the circled letter. Write down the letters in the spaces below as you go. Then use the Backward Alphabet Code with the key letter C to figure out the answer.

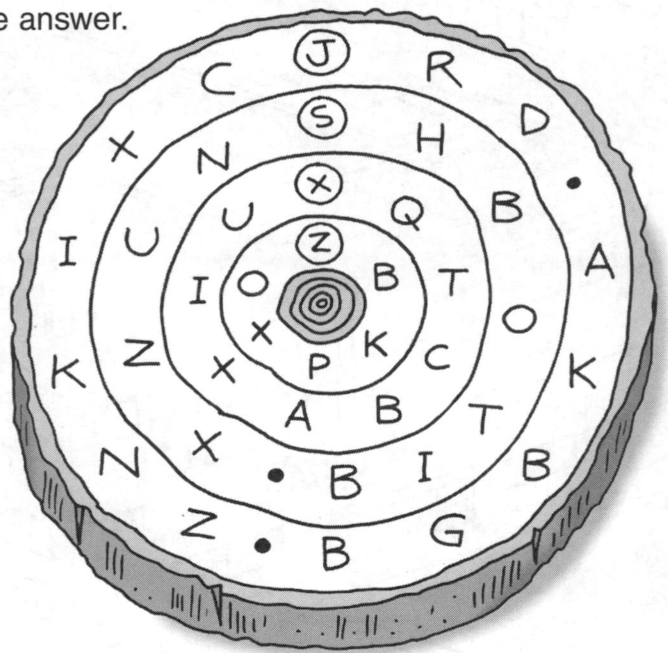


Letters: Z B A P X O  X Q T C P A X I U
S H B O J I B  _ _ _ _ _  _ _ _
_ _ _ _ _ _ _  _ _ _ _ _ _ _ _

Answer: _ _ _ _ _ _ _ _  _ _ _ _ _ _ _ _ _ _ _ _ _
_ _ _ _ _ _ _ _ _ _  _ _ _ _ _ _  _ _ _ _
_ _ _ _ _ _ _  _ _ _ _ _ _ _ _

# X-Ray Vision

Miss Gradenko has stolen a pair of spy glasses from the OSS. The spy glasses are receiving a coded message. Can you decipher the top secret information before she does? Color in all the triangles, then use the Backward Alphabet Code to crack the code.

Coded message:

GSV GSRIW Y ___ ___ ___ ___ ___ ___ ___ ___ ___ ___ ___ ___

Decoded message:

___ ___ ___   ___ ___ ___ ___ ___ ___   ___ ___ ___ ___ ___ ___   ___ ___ ___ ___ ___ ___

# CHAPTER FIVE:

## Your First Mission

**Secret Spy Tip #5:**

**"A Good Spy Has a Great Memory"**

You can crack any code, disappear in the blink of an eye, and you have gadgets for any situation hidden up your sleeve. But before you accept all those top secret missions about to come your way, here's one final test to make sure you're really spy material:

The Spy Kids are tearing apart Ukressa's Department Store, looking for Carmen and Juni. Study the scene on these two pages for a few minutes. Then turn to the next page and see how well you remember what you saw!

SPORTING
GOODS
GOLF
FIN
CHINA
ALL CDS
$5.00
CD
DISCOUNTS
UP
MUSIC
ROCK A–G
SPECIAL
BOOTS $200
BATH
SOAP
TOWELS
IMPORTED FROM THE TROPICS
$10

**Answer these questions after studying the picture on the two previous pages.**

1. How many Spy Kids are in the music department? 4
2. What is the Spy Kid at the top of the escalator holding? A man
3. Which department is above the music department? Sporting goods
4. Which letter is missing from the “Fine China” sign on the wall? E
5. How many Spy Kids are by the jewelry counter? 1
6. What are the Spy Kids doing in the music department? dancing
7. Does the escalator go up or down? Up
8. How much do the boots cost? ______
9. Where are the towels imported from? ______
10. What’s on tap at the snack shop? ______

***4 or more correct answers:*** Way to go! Quick, read the next page. The OSS is waiting to give you something.

***0-3 correct answers:*** Hmmm. You seem to be a little lacking in the spy skills department. Look over this book some more, and take the final quiz again. We’re sure you’ll do better next time!

# Congratulations!

You've passed the final round of spy training, and you are now a full-fledged spy. You are worthy of receiving the official Spy Kids certificate:

**This is to confirm that**

sethya
(code name)

**has passed all the necessary requirements for spying both here in**

Erope **and abroad.**
(name of country)

sethya
(code name)

**is hereby inducted into the ranks of counterintelligence throughout the world and can officially be sent on the next international OSS mission.**

date: 22' witnesses: Carmen Cortez
Carmen Cortez

Juni Cortez
Juni Cortez

# BONUS!

## A Super Spy Hunt

**Now that you're officially a secret agent, the best thing to do is to share your new spy knowledge with your friends. Then they can become secret agents too! Create your very own spy hunt to help your friends practice some secret agent ways.**

### HERE'S HOW TO CREATE A SPY HUNT YOU CAN PLAY IN YOUR OWN HOME

**Send your friends invitations** to find the top secret spy plans that are hidden in your house.

2

**Set up the trail beforehand**. Hide the "plans" somewhere difficult to find.

3

**Construct a set of clues for each player**. Each player should have the same number of clues, and each clue should tell the players where to find their next clue. Each player should have a different set of clues, but their last clue should take them to where the hidden plans are. Hide the clues around the house.

4

**When making up the clues...be creative!** Instead of writing a coded message that reads THE NEXT CLUE IS IN THE FRIDGE, word it this way: LOOK FOR THE NEXT CLUE AND HOP ON ONE LEG TO THE ONE PLACE YOU MIGHT FIND A HARD-BOILED EGG. (Code that rhyme, of course!) Or, if you hide a clue in your dresser drawer, try this clue: EVERY HIDING SPOT REALLY ROCKS, BUT THE NEXT ONE IS WHERE YOU'LL FIND MY SOCKS!

**Create a map for each player**. A simple sketch of the rooms in your house is a fun clue for your guests. The players can use the map to find one of the clues. For example, if you hide a clue on top of a chest of drawers, the previous clue should say something like:

> Walk into my bedroom
> Take three steps forward
> Take four steps to the right
> Take three steps to the left
> Reach up and feel around

**When your friends arrive, explain the tricks of the game**. Make the players familiar with the codes they will be using. Also give each player their own "spy kit" consisting of a pad of paper, pencils, and a Code Wheel (set to a certain letter).

**Play!** Hand out the first set of clues and watch as your friends take off to find the prize. You can walk around the house, giving anyone who's really stumped some help.

## Chapter One

### Hidden Clues (page 12):

1. He was hit in the chin too much
2. A gentleman is always kind.
3. Have you met my secretary?
4. Meet Mrs. Krasp, your new teacher.
5. In this winter scene, my snowman is huge!
6. An eagle, a duck, and a bear are at the zoo.
7. There is no operation today.
8. That railing is painted a strange color.
9. The bell next to Brad's ear chimed.
10. Who can work in this mess, a genius?

### Mission Control (page 13):

Carmen's code name: Sister Spy.
(shoe, tent, star, robot, egg, ice cream, pizza, sheep, yarn)

**I Spy** (page 14):

| | | | | | | | | | |
|---|---|---|---|---|---|---|---|---|---|
| S | S | E | E | S | I | P | S | S | S |
| S | P | I | S | I | P | S | P | I | I |
| P | I | P | I | S | E | S | S | E | S |
| S | S | S | P | P | S | E | I | S | P |
| I | S | S | S | I | S | P | I | S | I |
| E | E | P | E | P | S | S | S | I | E |
| S | S | I | E | I | S | P | E | P | P |
| S | P | S | S | E | P | E | I | S | P |
| S | S | I | P | S | I | S | P | E | S |
| E | P | S | E | S | E | P | I | P | I |

## **Word Games** (page 15):

7-letter words: PIGEONS, SEEPING

Some other words: PIGEON, SPONGE, PAGING, NOISE, POSING, GENES, SPINE SPAIN, SPIN, GAIN(S), SING, SANG, OPEN(S), SOAP, GONE, PINE(S), PAGE(S), NAPE, PAIN(S), SEEP(S), SAG(S), SEEN, SAGE, GAPE(S), ONE, POSE(S), SIGN(S), SNAP(S), NOSE(S), EASE(S), PEA(S), APE(S), PEN(S), PEG(S), PIN(S), PAN(S), GAS, GAP(S), NAP(S), NIP(S), PIE(S), PIG, IN, ON, AN, NO, IS, AS, GO

## **Kitchen Mission** (pages 16-17):

Hamburger, french fries, macaroni and cheese, spaghetti, fried chicken, rice and beans, tacos, peanut butter and jelly

The food goes in the: REHYDRATOR

# Chapter Two

## **Confidential: For Your Eyes Only** (page 28):

Ingrid's Secret: She shoots laser beams from under her fingernails.

Gregorio's Secret: He keeps a thin metal file hidden in his mustache.

## **Password Puzzler** (page 29):

Come close and you're toast, Pinhead!
Password: ACCESS DENIED

## **Picture This** (page 30-31):

The Third Brain is...
Behind a photograph

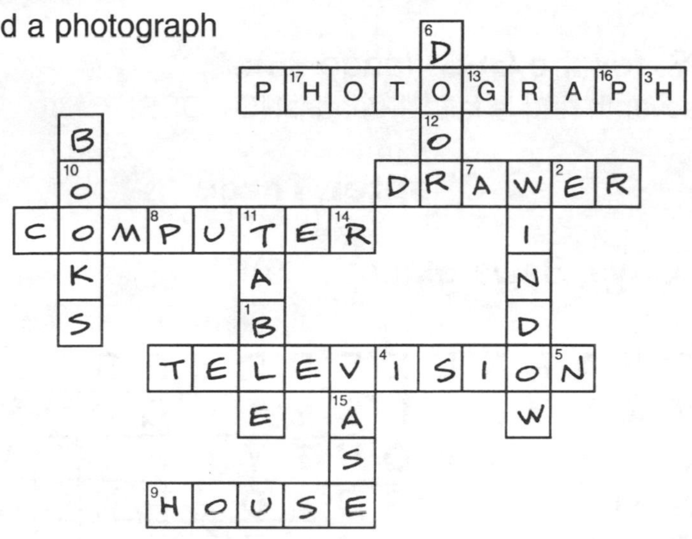


## **Tell It Like It Is** (page 32-33):

a. Searching for clues
b. You are under surveillance
c. Missing information
d. Double agent
e. They're after me
f. Double cross
g. Counterintelligence
h. Working undercover
i. Broken code
j. Disappearing ink
k. Decoder ring

**All Thumbs** (page 34):

The Thumb Thumbs love: FLOOP

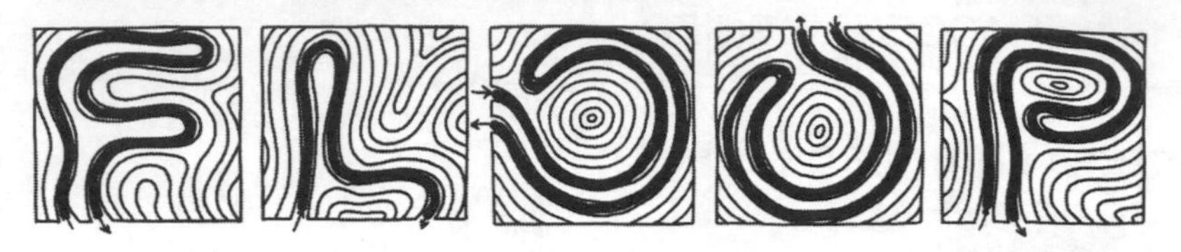

**S.O.S. for the OSS!** (page 35):

The seventh ring is fake. It reads: NOT OSS!

## Chapter Three

**Bad Guys, Beware!** (page 39):

| F | N | A | F | N | U | X | E | D | R | E | F | R | S | N |
|---|---|---|---|---|---|---|---|---|---|---|---|---|---|---|
| V | G | T | U | F | L | I | S | E | I | L | G | O | O | F |
| L | F | H | A | Y | A | Q | U | T | Y | F | H | I | P | A |
| N | I | M | I | S | S | G | R | A | D | E | N | K | O | A |
| O | O | N | S | M | M | N | G | U | R | I | G | Z | O | I |
| I | V | T | M | B | L | K | Q | C | M | I | F | G | L | S |
| T | N | U | B | M | M | F | E | R | T | S | Z | S | F | M |
| K | J | A | X | O | J | U | E | B | I | N | E | O | L | P |
| W | E | D | G | O | I | D | H | A | X | O | N | O | A | T |
| K | R | N | E | F | N | H | F | T | O | N | D | P | H | S |
| N | G | A | F | A | G | P | N | K | B | O | O | C | E | T |
| O | F | L | X | X | P | S | I | L | R | M | R | Q | F | U |
| I | B | E | N | A | N | X | E | D | E | F | U | F | W | V |
| M | L | D | W | O | I | E | X | A | Z | E | F | H | A | D |
| A | C | D | E | R | M | P | Y | L | N | G | E | B | T | X |

## Will the Real Carmen Please Stand Up? (page 40):

The real Carmen is #2

## Super Guppy Getaway (page 41):

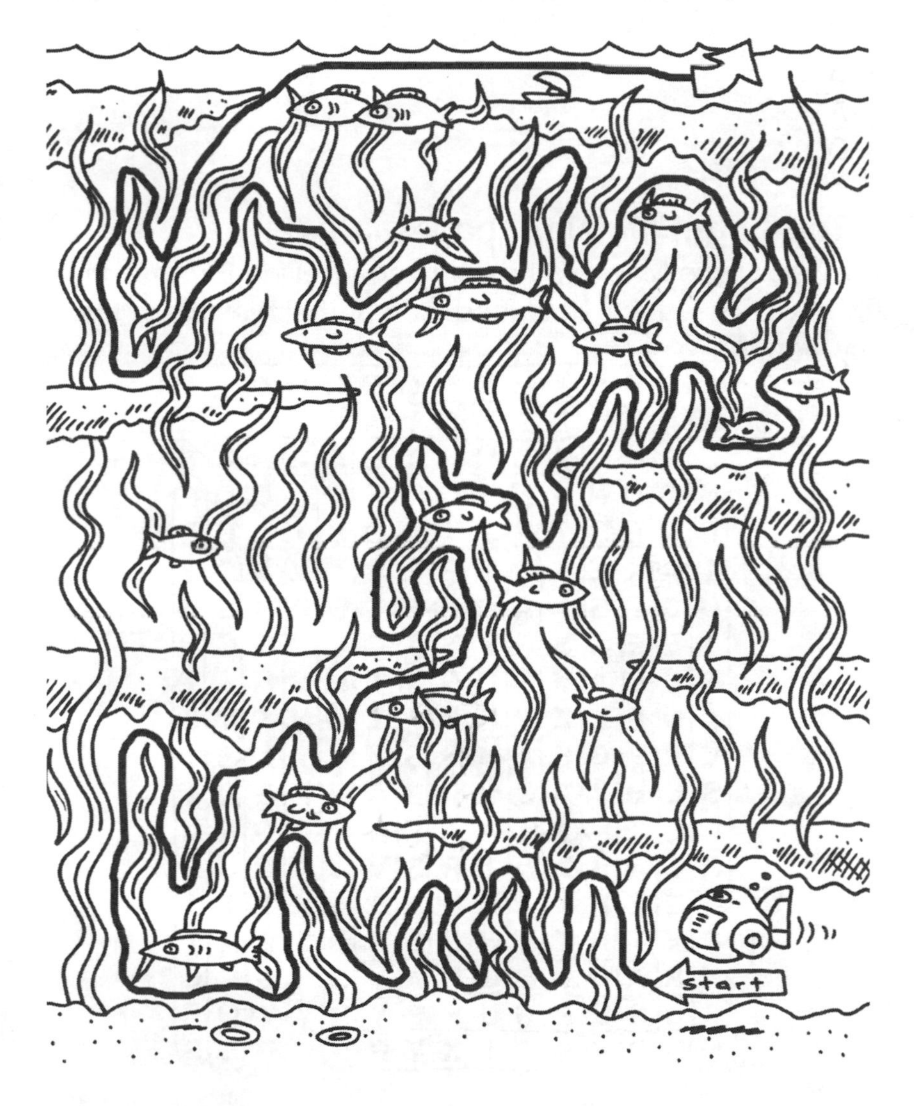

## **Now You See It, Now You Don't** (page 44):

Hold the book parallel to the ground (with the pages facing up) about a foot away from your nose.
The message reads: YOU'RE FIRED

## **Cable Collision** (page 45):

1. C
2. B
3. A
4. D

## **A Top-Flight Mission** (pages 46–47):

Answer: Uncle Machete has only one Beijing Express in his spy shop—the fastest land, sea and air vehicle in the spy world!

**Danger Ahead!** (page 48):
A shark is in their way.

**Thumbs Up!** (page 49):

## Chapter Four

**Codes From A-Z** (page 61):
Message: A good spy always uses codes

**The Ultimate Brain Baffler** (page 61):
Answer: THE ENEMY (N+M+E)

**TV Signals** (page 61):
HELP US!

## Double Trouble (pages 62-63):

On Ukressas's: They're headed for the library.
On the Library: Check the hospital next.
On the Hospital: Meet me at the supermarket.
On the supermarket:
Had to go. I'm headed for the police station.
On the police station: I see them at the playground.
At the playround: I found them!
The robot doubles were hiding at the playground.

## The Name of the Game (page 64):

answer: Carmen Elizabeth Juanita Echo Sky Brava Cortez

## X-Ray Vision (page 65):

Message: The Third Brain lives

# Chapter Five

## Memory Test (page 68):

1. Four
2. A salesman (or man)
3. Sporting Goods
4. E
5. Two
6. Dancing
7. Up
8. $200
9. The tropics
10. Soda pop